Squeak Street

Old Bun
and the Burglar

Squeak Street stories
by Emily Rodda

Old Bun and the Burglar
One-Shoe's Wishes
Fee-Fee's Holiday
Pink-Paw's Painting

Old Bun
and the Burglar

Illustrated by
Andrew McLean

HAPPY CAT BOOKS

Meet the mice who live in Squeak Street

Old Bun lives in Number One.
His piles of gold shine like the sun.

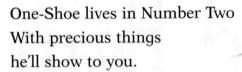

One-Shoe lives in Number Two
With precious things
he'll show to you.

Fee-Fee lives in Number Three
With her enormous family.

Pink-Paw lives in Number Four.
She paints until her paws are sore.

Fat Clive cooks in Number Five.
He makes us glad to be alive.

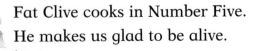

Quick-Sticks lives in Number Six.
Her band is called the Squeaky Chicks.

Kevin lives in Number Seven.
He thinks old cars
are simply heaven.

Tails the Great, in Number Eight,
Spooks us into an awful state.

Adeline, in Number Nine,
Builds boats — all to her own design.

And post-mouse Ben, in Number Ten,
Is resting his poor feet again.

Published by
Happy Cat Books
An imprint of Catnip Publishing Ltd
Islington Business Centre
3-5 Islington High Street
London N1 9LQ

First published in Australia 2006 by Working Title Press,
33 Balham Avenue, Kingswood, SA 5062

This edition first published 2007
1 3 5 7 9 10 8 6 4 2

A CIP catalogue record for this book is available
from the British Library

ISBN 978-1-905117-51-2

Printed in Poland

www.catnippublishing.co.uk

Contents

~

Chapter 1
~
The Letter

Old Bun was very, very rich. All the front rooms of his grand house at Number One Squeak Street were filled with piles of golden cheese.

Old Bun loved looking at his cheese and smelling its rich perfume.

He loved showing it to visitors.

And he loved sharing it with friends. His cheese-tasting parties were famous in Squeak Street.

Old Bun also loved getting letters, especially letters from his grandchildren, who lived on the other side of Mouseville.

One night, Old Bun was sitting in his living room, feeling a bit lonely.

Ben the post-mouse hadn't called on him that day, so he had no new letters to cheer him up. His servants had all gone home. He kept hearing strange little sounds that made him nervous.

He hobbled over to the front door, to make sure that it was locked. And there, lying on the floor just inside the door, was a letter!

Old Bun was thrilled.

"I had a letter today after all!" he said. "Well, bless my whiskers! Ben must have been very late, so he just pushed it under the door."

He bent stiffly and picked the letter up. It looked important. The words VERY URGENT were printed at the top.

"Urgent!" Old Bun exclaimed. His heart was beating fast as he tore the letter open.

He read the note inside.

WARNING TO ALL RICH OLD MICE
WHO LIVE ALONE!
BURGLARS are at work in Mouseville
Many RICH OLD MICE have already been
ROBBED OF ALL THEY OWN!
your ONLY HOPE is to find THREE
STRONG GUARDS to protect you.
DO IT NOW! before it is
TOO LATE!!!

By the time Old Bun had finished reading the letter, he was so afraid that his fur was standing on end.

He looked around his cosy living room, and his beautiful, shining piles of cheese.

He imagined the room cold and bare, and all the cheese gone. He imagined himself a poor mouse, with no food, no piles of gold — perhaps not even a bed to sleep in!

Panic gripped him.

He had no idea how to find even *one* strong guard. No idea at all.

And, just then, there was a loud knock on the door.

Chapter 2
~
The Guards

Old Bun crept to the door.

"Who is it?" he asked nervously.

"Rich Mouse Guard Company," a loud voice answered. "Do you need three strong guards, by any chance?"

Amazed, Old Bun opened the door.

Outside stood three of the biggest mice he had ever seen. They wore dark sunglasses and smart blue uniforms. They looked very strong.

Old Bun almost fainted with joy. "Please come in!" he cried.

He sprang back to stop himself being crushed as the big mice marched into the house.

"I'm Red," the largest guard said. "These guys are Fang and Claw."

Fang and Claw were gazing at Old Bun's cheese and grinning.

"We'll need a truck," Claw muttered.

Red kicked him hard on the ankle.

"A truck?" asked Old Bun, confused.

"Not truck, sir, *luck*," said Red loudly. "It was a bit of *luck* that we just happened to be passing. We love helping rich old mice like you. Right, team?"

"Right," Fang and Claw agreed. And it was true that they looked very happy indeed.

Red rubbed his hands. "Now," he said. "First, we'll have a snack, to keep up our strength. Then we'll get to work."

After the snack, which was very large, Claw went out. He said he had to see a sick friend.

Then, to Old Bun's horror, Red and Fang began moving his cheese!

He tried to stop them, but they took no notice. Puffing and panting, they cleared the living room, the bedrooms, the games room and the library.

They carried all the golden piles off to the back of the house.

"Our cheese — I mean, *your* cheese — will be safer in one place, sir," Red said. "That big room beside the back door is the cheese room now."

"But I never use the back room. My legs are too weak to walk that far," Old Bun wailed. "And how can visitors see my gold if it's locked away?"

"Visitors?" Red snorted loudly. "There'll be no more visitors here, eating everything they can lay their paws on!"

He stuck a **KEEP OUT** sign on the front door. Then he locked the door, and put the key in his pocket.

"But how will my servants get in tomorrow?" protested Old Bun.

Red grinned. "You don't need servants any more, old mouse," he said. "You've got us. Now, you just toddle off to bed. We'll take care of everything."

Chapter 3

~

The Cheese Room

The hours went by. Old Bun lay awake. He was miserable.

He missed his cheese. His bedroom looked very empty without it. And also, he was hungry. He hadn't had a snack for hours.

He got out of bed, crept to the bedroom door and peeped out. Red and Fang were playing cards in the living room, talking in low voices.

Old Bun decided not to disturb them, in case Red sent him back to bed. He was sick of being bossed around in his own house.

He lit a candle. Then, very quietly, he set off down the hallway.

It was a long, long way to the cheese room. Only the delicious smell of his cheese, growing stronger, gave Old Bun the strength to keep going.

He had just begun to feel that his poor legs were too weak to carry him any further, when at last he reached the back of the house.

A wonderful, rich perfume rose from the crack under the cheese room door. Old Bun opened the door and crept inside.

The door swung shut behind him. There was a sudden scuffling sound. A huge shadow rose black against the wall.

"Oh, great cheese!" Old Bun said to himself in terror. "A burglar!"

"Help!" he croaked.

"Help!" wailed the burglar.

Old Bun blinked. The burglar's shadow was huge, but the burglar himself was very small.

"You don't look like a burglar," said Old Bun.

"I'm *not* a burglar," sobbed the burglar. "I'm Bert. I only came in here to sleep, like I do every night. I've got no home, and it's cold outside."

"Every night?" exclaimed Old Bun. "But how do you get in?"

Bert pointed to the window that faced the back street. "That window is always open," he sniffed. "And no one ever comes here. But tonight two scary rats in sunglasses came, with all this cheese. I hid, but — "

"They aren't rats!" cried Old Bun, very shocked. "They're my guards!"

"They looked like rats to me," snuffled Bert. "When they'd gone I tried to get away, but they'd shut the window. It was too heavy for me to lift. I was trapped! And now you've found me here. You'll call the police!"

He burst into tears again.

And, just then, there was a loud rumbling noise in the road outside.

Chapter 4
~
No Escape

Old Bun looked out the window. He saw that a truck had stopped at the back door. Claw was in the driver's seat.

And at that moment, Old Bun saw the terrible truth.

"Oh, what a fur-brained fool I've been!" he groaned.

"What's the matter?" asked Bert timidly.

"My guards aren't guards at all," Old Bun moaned. "They're robbers!"

He pulled his ears in misery. "I see it all now," he said. "They put that letter under my door. They tricked me. And now they're going to take all my cheese away in that truck."

Bert's eyes were very wide. "You mean those scary rats will be coming back?" he whispered. "To get the cheese?"

"Yes," Old Bun said. His heart had begun to pound. "They'll be here any minute. And if they find us here ..."

In panic, he heaved at the window. It opened, just a little.

"Get away, Bert!" he said. "Run!"

"But what about you?" asked Bert.

"My legs are too weak to climb out of windows," snapped Old Bun. "And the gap's too small for me, anyway. Go! Save yourself!"

With a sob, Bert scrambled out of the window, and disappeared into the darkness.

Claw didn't notice. He was too busy knocking on the back door.

After a while, Old Bun heard the sound of feet padding down the hallway. He heard the back door creaking open. He heard Red's harsh voice.

"You took your time! Let's load the stuff and get out of here."

"What about the old mouse?" growled Claw.

"He's asleep," Red said. "If he stays asleep, we'll leave him alone. Otherwise ..."

Fang giggled nastily.

Old Bun shivered, and slid down behind a huge pile of cheese. Peering around it, he saw the door of the cheese room swing open.

Red stood there, with Fang and Claw behind him.

"Oh, well, I've had a good life," Old Bun said to himself. "I'm only sorry it had to end like this."

Then, suddenly, a terrible din began in the street.

Chapter 5
~
"Help, Police!"

Red, Claw and Fang turned and ran outside.

Trembling, Old Bun stood up and peeped out of the window.

He was amazed to see that the street was full of mice in pyjamas.

All the Squeak Street mice were there, shouting at the tops of their voices: "Help, police! Police!"

And that wasn't all.

Quick-Sticks, from Number Six, was beating a drum.

Fat Clive, from Number Five, was banging a cake pan with a spoon.

Fee-Fee, from Number Three, was ringing a dinner bell, and all her children were blowing toy trumpets ...

Everyone had found an extra way to make a noise. The sound was deafening!

In terror, Old Bun saw Red, Fang and Claw grabbing at his friends, trying to catch them. Red, Fang and Claw were big and strong, and very angry.

But the Squeak Street mice were fast. They ducked and ran, and the noise went on.

Then another sound rose above the rest.

It was the sound of a siren, coming closer. The police had heard the din, and were on their way.

"Let's get out of here!" Old Bun heard Red shout.

The gang jumped into the truck.

Mice scattered, cheering, as the truck roared away. They cheered again as three cars full of police arrived. And again as the police set off after the truck.

Then everyone came into Old Bun's house. They moved all the cheese back to where it belonged as Old Bun thanked them again and again.

"It's this brave young mouse you really have to thank," said Fee-Fee, pushing little Bert forward. "Instead of running away, he crept from door to door, and woke us all up. Is he one of your grandsons?"

Old Bun shook his head. "No," he said. "He's ... he's my new guard, as a matter of fact. He's going to live here, in Number One, from now on, to keep an eye on things. Aren't you, Bert?"

"Yes, please," said Bert, his face shining.

Old Bun felt very happy. Everything was perfect.

Except for one thing.

He looked around at all his friends. "I'm starving!" he said. "Let's have a midnight feast!"

And so they did.